GAHAN WILSON'S

GRAVEDIGGERS' PARTY

GAHAN WILSON'S
GRAVEDIGGERS' PARTY

GAHAN WILSON

ibooks

new york
www.ibooks.net

DISTRIBUTED BY SIMON & SCHUSTER, INC

To Paul

A Publication of ibooks, inc.

Copyright © 2002 Gahan Wilson

An ibooks, inc. Book

Distributed by Simon & Schuster, Inc.
1230 Avenue of the Americas, New York, NY 10020

ibooks, inc.
24 West 25th Street
New York, NY 10010

The ibooks World Wide Web Site Address is:
http://www.ibooks.net

ISBN 0-7434-4548-1
First ibooks, inc. printing October 2002
10 9 8 7 6 5 4 3 2 1

Edited by Steven A. Roman

Cover art copyright © 2002 Gahan Wilson

Cover design and color by Mike Rivilis
Interior design by Joe Bailey

Printed in the U.S.A.

GRAVEDIGGERS' PARTY
An Introduction by Gahan Wilson

A cartoon is as durable as the Frankenstein monster.

Once printed, it is almost impossible to be completely destroyed, because every last copy of the magazine in which it was originally printed must be thoroughly pulped, not to mention every edition of every anthology it has managed to sneak into thereafter, and even then it can insidiously lurk on through generations and the collapse of societies such as ours if only one refined person of taste is kind enough to slip just a single clipping of it between the pages of a book or tack it onto the beam of a reasonably waterproof attic.

But, in the same way that the Frankenstein monster cannot ravage quaint, middle-European villages, or flip peasants' innocent, young daughters into lakes so long as he is imprisoned in the charred ruins of a collapsed windmill, no cartoon can possibly share its joke with deserving people such as yourself so long as it's bound into a moldering magazine which, in turn, is locked inside a long-forgotten trunk.

For that reason, at great risk to both my sanity and health, I have, with considerable trepidation, fumbled through the mold-greened pages of numerous extinct periodicals; risked more than likely exposure to the Hantavirus in the dark, ill-ventilated basements of shady book dealers. I was more than glad to do so because it seemed to me—in spite of all the heartbreak and sacrifice which were required—it was my simple duty to see to it that these little lost cartoons were disinterred from the paper tombs and crypts in which they have lain helpless for far too long a time and set free again to romp and gambol in a brand new book.

So here they are, bless their hearts, all of them ready and willing to make you smile—hopefully a little nervously—each eagerly rubbing their tiny, clattering claws together and licking their sharp little teeth, and I can assure you that every single one of the little rascals can hardly wait to party.

Thank you for joining them—and have a good time!

"Didn't everybody used to have faces?"

"Kill!"

"Kill!"

"No fair turning yourself off, Mr. Hasbrow!"

"Harry, I wish you'd stop *doing* that!"

"Alright. Now exhale."

9

"Poor Fifi hasn't been the same since the veterinarian put
the brain of his hunchbacked assistant into her skull!"

"And everyday it's costing more and more!"

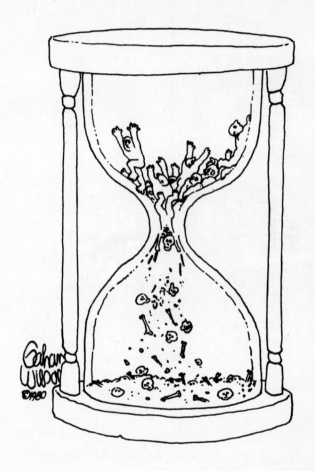

"Dump all my shares of Peabody and Fenner!"

"Where are the others?"

Gahan Wilson

*"There's another one of those abominable
mountain climbers."*

"Well, I guess that pretty well takes care of my
anemia diagnosis."

"Excuse me for shouting—
I thought you were farther away."

"In here."

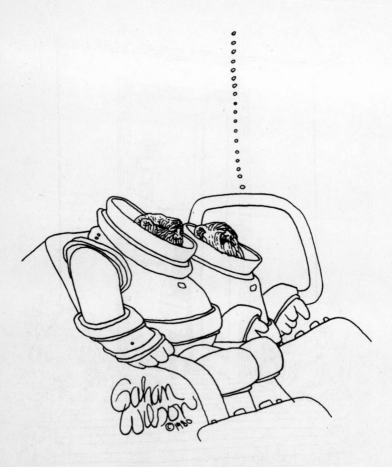

"Well, it won't be long, now!"

"One day, when he's old and feeble, he'll be in a nostalgic mood, and he'll come up here to see us again, and to reminisce— _and_ _then_ _we'll_ _get_ _him!_"

"It wasn't *always* like this with me..."

"Nothing personal, Dad, but if I were you, I wouldn't ask too
many questions about my boy's club."

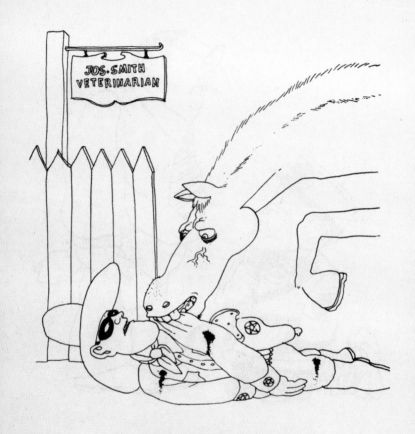

"No, big fellow, you must take me
to a *people* doctor!"

"Hello! You have reached the number of Harold Mayberry. I am sorry, but Mr. Mayberry is not in. I am a simulation of Mr. Mayberry. Please leave your name and number and Mr. Mayberry will call you back when he gets in. Thank you very much!"

FAKE
IT.

Gahan Wilson

27

"Our people have many sayings on
the vanity of haste, effendi..."

"Oh, that Harry's so jealous!"

"I'm sorry, young man, I just can't go through
with this ceremony."

"How did you come to name your boat the Revenge, Captain?"

" . . . And now point out the man you saw murder Miss La Rue!"

"That's tone control. The volume's up there."

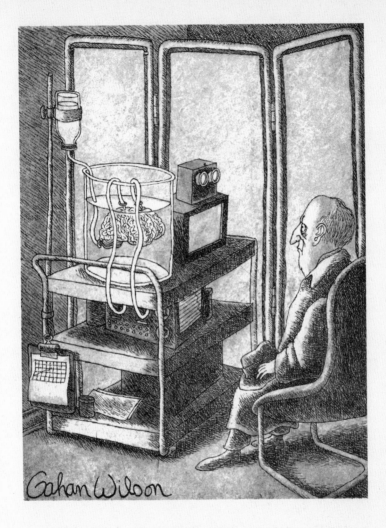

"The doctors . . . say . . . they've never . . . seen . . . another case quite . . . like . . . it."

"How come we draw all the shaggy dog cases?"

"I always knew the kid
had a lot of guts!"

"Well, that's the story of Little Red Riding Hood and the Wolf.
Would you like to hear another?"

"*Easy on the fast balls, will you, kid?*"

"It's me!"

"Just who do you think you're talking to?"

"Now that you've come of age, son, I think it's time your old dad let you in on our little family curse."

"This is the place, driver."

Gahan Wilson

"I think we've located the cause of that tie-up at
Thirty-fourth Street and Seventh Avenue!"

"You fool! There's no more of me!
That's it! I'm the last of my species!"

"I don't know, Professor, this civilization is so primitive,
it hardly seems worth our time!"

"It's been awful for business, Mrs. Schultz, but
it was Charlie's last wish."

"Straight ahead, Bernie, dear."

"Hold it, Charlie."

"The sandwich-man killer has struck again!"

Gahan
Wilson

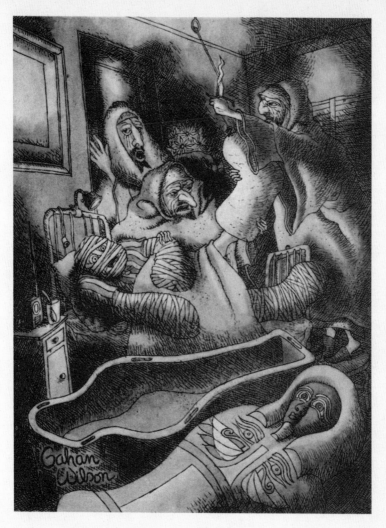

"I tell you guys, you're making a horrible mistake!"

"So what the hell do we do *now*?"

"Will you shut up with that screaming!"

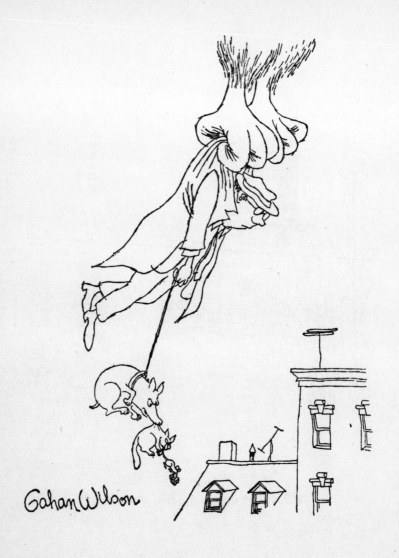

Gahan Wilson

62

"I wish you wouldn't worry so much about me, George.
After all, I'm only a figment of your imagination."

"Harry, I really think you ought to go to the doctor."

"See what I mean? No matter how many times I pull
its trigger, the damned thing just won't fire!"

"This is about that raise, I suppose?"

"We may already be too late, Mr. Parker."

"You spit out Dr. Harper this very minute!"

"Look—I've really *got* to leave."

"For God's sake, Leona, why don't you just finish me off?"

"That one holds Ezra's love letters and this one holds Ezra."

"Of course, once the plague's done, we're both out a job."

"I *knew* this would happen if those damned
conservationists had their way!"

"It all worked out just as you said it would, mother!"

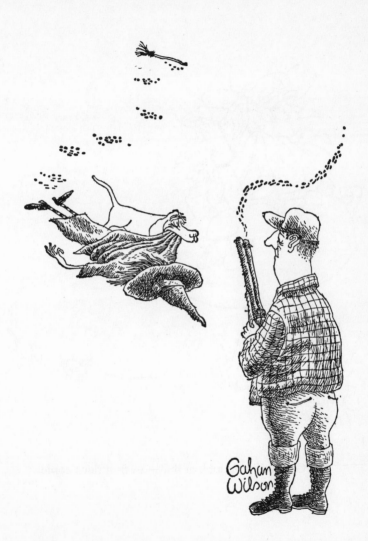

"By God, will you look at that— even littler people!"

"It's no good—I'm out here, too!"

"My God—you don't mean
it's *still* 1935?"

"I think you would be well advised to locate
the new delphinium bed elsewhere, Hobbs."

"...And if they won't do it for me then strike them dead with a lightning bolt like you did with Uncle Sherman."

"Damn it—I _told_ them I was too well known for undercover work."

"It's here, again, Henri!"

"Get your hands off me, Madame."

"My goodness, Mr. Merryweather, we certainly _did_ make
a boo-boo with that prescription of yours!"

"Where are you *taking* me?"

"You don't get rid of him that easy, Mrs. Jacowsky."

"When did you first become aware of this imagined
'plot to get you,' Mr. Potter?"

Gahan Wilson

"I only said you could take it with you.
I didn't say you could keep it!"

"This isn't going to help, Edward."

"Look, what can I tell you? That's the head
of network programming."

"I paint what I see, child."

"Oh, you see both sides to *everything*!"

"How much for just the ring?"

"I'm <u>sure</u> of it, Harry—it's that nice
Mr. Bently we met on the tour!"

"Look, Mr. Tompkins, there is simply nothing
I can do for you after you're dead!"

"The Boston Strangler!"
"Frankenstein Meets the Wolfman?"
"Breathless?"
"Something by Shakespeare?"

"I know this will be a disappointment to you, Mr. Barton, but you're in excellent health and will probably live for many, many years to come."

"I think we may be just the store for you, sir!"

"We're city little people, lady, if it's
any of your damn business."

"To hell with *this* stuff!"

"Apparently we're not the first one..."

"Here she comes again, and she's got another poodle!"

"There you are, you naughties!"

"I figure everybody else is doing it."

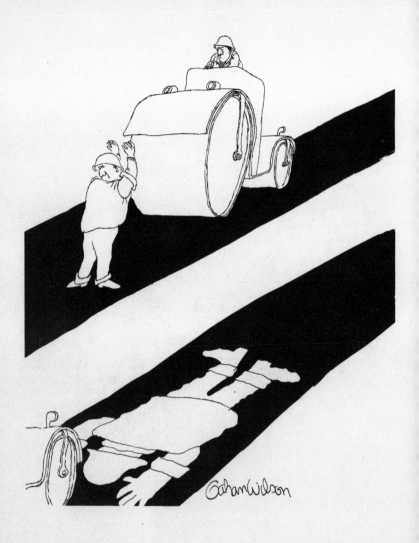

"Sir! The Moorne Castle Monster is under the strict protection of the National Historical Trust!"

"My _goodness_, how he's grown!"

"It's a good thing Effie likes these funerals,
she's had such awful luck with her pets."

"Accursed daylight saving time!"

"There's obviously been some sort of ghastly mistake!"

"Hi, gang, glad you dropped by our sprightly nightly,
'cause I think this P.M. we're going to have even more fun than usual!"

"Gee—it's just like in the movies!"

"You're really crazy about that girl, aren't you, kid?"

CAT
RAT
HAT

Gahan
Wilson

131

"Does this mean it's all over between us, Harvey?"

"Seems all we ever do is complain!"

". . . and, for what it's worth, my blessing."

"Oh, Irwin, I wish to God you'd get rid of that thing!"

SOON ON THIS SITE
THE
J.B. ROTHMAN
ELEMENTARY
SCHOOL
CONSTRUCTED
FOR THE CITY
BY THE
ACME
CONSTRUCTION
COMPANY

Gahan Wilson

"Life is like . . . ah . . . life is . . . uhm . . . like . . . er . . .
life is like a dream!"

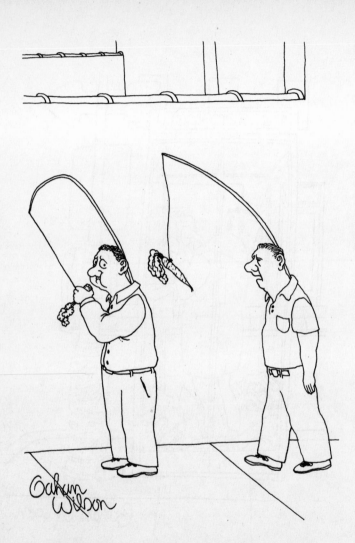

"Alright, then—*now* what are you going to do?"

"My God—do you suppose it can read?!"

"Look, Mr. Gurney, let's not kid ourselves.
Crazy is crazy."

"Fred, I think you're spending altogether too much
time down here with these mushrooms!"

"Thank you. And my friend's is made of rough canvas
and has leather straps sewn into it."

"We'll never get anywhere with these
constant interruptions from the front!"

"So far, all the tests indicate, as we feared, that
you *are* a cocker spaniel."

"Over here, for God's sake!"

"Yeah? Well, they don't make *me* feel insignificant, fellah!"

"Damned hard luck, Fitzhue."

"I'm afraid this simulator test indicates Commodore Brent
would be a poor choice for the Lunar Expedition."

"Sorry to keep you so late, but I'm determined to get to the bottom of this werewolf fixation of yours."

"When was it you decided to become a bad guy, Ed?"

"You funnin' me, bub?"

"Ha ha Bill."
"Ha ha George."
"Ha ha. And here's Harry ha ha with the sports.
  Ha ha Harry."
"Ha ha George."

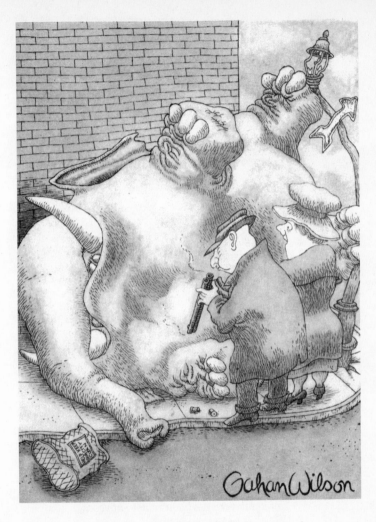

"Honestly, Harry, I'll never tease you again for
carrying around that elephant gun!"

"You know very well you're not supposed
to beg at the table!"

"Hold it, Newton. We've been barking up the wrong tree."

"Confound it, staff <u>knows</u> this door's to be kept locked!"

Gahan Wilson

" . . . Only a minute or so more and man will have his
first view of the other side of the moon!"

"Don't you worry, Mr. Kiernan—we'll have you out of there in no time!"

"... is pleased to announce a complete and devastating victory
over the enemy. This is a recorded message.
The government is pleased. . . ."

"*Congratulations, Baer—I think you've wiped out the species!*"

ABOUT THE AUTHOR

GAHAN WILSON says, "I was born dead, and this helped my career almost as much as being the nephew of a lion tamer and a descendant of P.T. Barnum." The first confessed cartoonist to graduate from the Art Institute of Chicago, Wilson has shown at galleries in New York and San Francisco, and his genius for humor has been likened by critics

to that of Swift, Gogol and Twain. His work has appeared in *The New Yorker*, *Paris Match*, *Playboy*, *Punch*, *Twilight Zone* magazine, *The National Lampoon*, and *The New York Times*.